A Horse Called Deathblow

Tudor stories linking in with the
National Curriculum Key Stage 2

This edition 2008

Franklin Watts
338 Euston Road
London
NW1 3BH

Franklin Watts Australia
Level 17/207 Kent Street
Sydney NSW 2000

Series editor: Paula Borton
Consultant: Joan Blyth
Designer: Kirstie Billingham

A CIP catalogue record for this book
is available from the British Library.

ISBN: 978 0 7496 8502 7

Dewey Classification: 942.05

Printed in Great Britain by CPI Cox & Wyman, Reading, RG1 8EX

Franklin Watts is a division of Hachette Children's Books,
an Hachette Livre UK company.
www.hachettelivre.co.uk

A Horse Called Deathblow

by
Karen Wallace

Illustrations by Martin Remphry

W
FRANKLIN WATTS
LONDON•SYDNEY

To Ned

1

The Wrong Side of the Bed

Arthur Knucklebone stumbled up the staircase with a tray in one hand and a big wooden bucket in the other. Hot water slopped from the bucket and soaked his feet. Arthur stopped to catch his breath.

Ten minutes before, he had been

 standing in the kitchen waiting for his orders when the Master of the Household burst into the room clutching a breakfast tray. He bellowed for the Royal Groom.

But the Royal Groom was nowhere to be found! The Master had stared wild-eyed around the kitchen and caught sight of Arthur edging into the shadows.

Now Arthur shifted the heavy bucket to his other hand, being careful not to drop

the tray.
A prickle of
sweat broke
out on his
brow.
Because the

tray he was carrying was King Henry
VIII's breakfast tray. And mornings in the
Royal Household could sometimes be a
bit *difficult*.

From behind a heavy oak door at the
top of the stairs there was a loud groan.
Something heavy landed with a *thud* on
the floor.

"Breakfast, Sire," said Arthur, as he
walked into the King's bedchamber. He
put the bucket on the floor and laid the
tray on the table at the end of the King's
huge four poster bed.

Arthur's stomach rumbled loudly. He tried not to look at the the bowl of creamy porridge, the moist pink pigeon pie, a plump apple dumpling sitting in its pool of lemon syrup and the tankard of strong ale.

"Go away!" muttered the King. "I'm not hungry."

"It's your favourite, Sire" said Arthur in his cheeriest voice. Then he saw the

8

upturned books and the hand-held mirrors that lay in pieces on the floor.

Arthur sighed. It was going to be one of those *difficult* mornings.

Suddenly a jewelled hand appeared through the bed hangings, and a portrait flew past Arthur's head and landed with a crash on the floor.

A second later the hangings were ripped

back. "Well?" demanded King Henry, his mouth full of pigeon pie. "What do you think?"

Arthur Knucklebone looked at the portrait in its smashed frame on the floor. It was of a young man who looked very similar to Henry. Except that he had dark brown hair, and Henry's was red.

Arthur knew he had to say something, but he wasn't sure what it should be.

And he certainly
didn't want to
get it wrong.

He decided
on the direct
approach.

"Who is he?" said Arthur.

"The new king of France," said Henry
gloomily. "Is he handsomer than me?"
The King looked deep into Arthur's face.
"Tell me the *truth*," he said. "I want your
honest opinion."

Arthur had worked for King Henry long
enough to know that honest opinions were
extremely bad for your health. He put his
hand to his neck. He wanted to keep his
neck just where it was. Attached to his
shoulders, that is.

The King pulled his nightgown to his

knees and planted a bare foot on the end of the bed. "No leg could be shapelier than mine," he yelled.

"No, Sire," agreed Arthur, carefully.

"I am the *greatest* King in Europe, aren't I, Arthur?" moaned Henry VIII.

"Yes Sire," replied Arthur.

"But now I don't *feel* like the greatest king in Europe," groaned King Henry.

"What am I going to do?"

"Do, Sire?"

"There's a big tournament today," howled King Henry. "Everybody will be there. And they'll all be watching *me*."

"They will?" said Arthur.

"They will," cried the King. "And it's all Cardinal Wolsey's fault."

"It is?" said Arthur.

"It is," cried King Henry. "Just because he's chief minister, he thinks he knows best. He said if everyone sees I'm the greatest jouster, then they'll think England is the greatest *country*. So he talked me into it."

"Into what?"

"Into jousting against the Champion Jouster of All France," said the King. "To show how *great* I am. And there's to be a

huge banquet
afterwards to
celebrate."

"But you're
the greatest
jouster in the
land," said
Arthur. "The
best, the bravest,
the - "

But the
King wasn't listening. "Now, that
stupid portrait has ruined *everything.*" He
sniffed. "*And* I'm getting a cold." Henry
stared at Arthur Knucklebone. "So,
Arthur," he said, his voice rising. "Tell me
the truth. Is the French King more
handsome than me?"

Arthur Knucklebone thought fast. It just

so happened his mother, Old Mother Knucklebone, was visiting London. She had taken to reading the future and telling fortunes. And she was good at it. Because Old Mother Knucklebone knew *exactly* what people wanted to hear and made sure she told them just that.

"I'm *w-a-i-t-i-n-g,* Arthur," said the King in a nasty voice.

Arthur gulped. "I don't know, Sire," he began. "But - "

"You don't know!" roared the King.

"*But* I do know someone who does," said Arthur, quickly.

"Excellent," cried the King in a happy voice. "Who is this person?"

"Old Mother Knucklebone," said Arthur, bowing. "She's, er, a relation."

The King jumped out of bed and yanked open the door. "Send for Old Mother Knucklebone!" he bellowed.

Two minutes later, there was a knock on the door and a man dressed in long red robes and a red hat glided into the room.

It was Cardinal Wolsey. The King's smile disappeared.

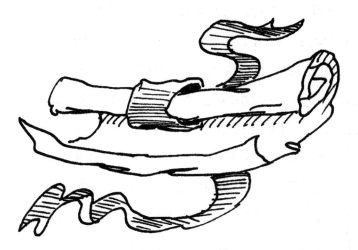

2

The Bones Never Lie

Cardinal Wolsey was a stubby man with a heavy-jowled face and dark, clever eyes. He had the slinking, cautious walk of a man used to dodging trouble.

"What do you mean by interrupting my breakfast?" yelled the King.

Cardinal Wolsey bowed and held out a parchment scroll. "Carp, capon, stork, eels, gannet, pullets, partridge," he droned as if he was reading a sermon. "Would His Majesty like a seal?"

"A seal? A seal?" shouted King Henry. Then he raised his eyebrows and smirked at Arthur. "Do think he means a *seal of approval?*" he asked, slowly.

It was a joke. Actually, thought Arthur, it was quite a good joke as far as the King's jokes went. He laughed lightly. Wolsey, on the other hand, rolled about the floor, giggling uncontrollably.

"Devilishly droll, Sire," he sobbed, wiping a tear away.

"Get up, Wolsey," snapped Henry.

"It wasn't *that* funny." His eyes glittered. "And stop pestering me about menus. You know seal gives me indigestion."

"I beg your pardon, Sire," replied Cardinal Wolsey. "I just thought -"

"I don't care what you think," interrupted the King. "Just make sure there are lots of jellies." King Henry stamped his foot. "I like jellies!" he yelled.

Cardinal Wolsey bowed. "I have appointed a Gentleman-of-the-Jellies," he said in an even voice. "One George McWhibble. A famous Scottish jelly maker and a craftsman in his field."

"At least you've done *something* right," muttered the King.

Cardinal Wolsey bowed and glided towards the door as if he was on wheels.

Arthur was delighted. George McWhibble was a friend of his. They had met in the kitchens under the palace when Arthur had just arrived from the country with his pet pig. Of course, Henry the pig was no longer with Arthur. The Spanish Ambassador had been so impressed with his tricks that in the interests of world peace, King Henry had reluctantly agreed to send him to Spain.

Arthur sighed. It all seemed a long time ago, now. Indeed, it was almost the last time he had seen his mother, Old Mother Knucklebone.

"Who's that ugly Frog in the painting?" screeched a voice like a crow.

An old woman with a beaky face had suddenly appeared in the room. She stood staring at the smashed portrait.

"Look at his hair," she squawked. "Thin
as old rags. And legs like tree trunks."

Henry's face lit up. He turned to Arthur.
"Who is this wise and gifted woman," he
demanded. It was almost as if Old Mother
Knucklebone had been hiding under the
bed all the time. She reached into her skirt
and held out a small jar. "Best thing for a

cold," she croaked. "Spider in treacle. Works every time."

King Henry's eyes were round as pewter plates.

"Your Majesty," Arthur said. "May I present Old Mother Knucklebone, fortune teller to the famous?"

"Enchanted," cried King Henry.

Old Mother Knucklebone curtseyed and pulled at a pouch that hung at her waist. "The bones," she said. "The bones will tell us what the future holds." She poured a pile of little bones into her cupped hand and rattled them.

The King was delighted. "Arthur," he cried, "this glorious woman and I have much to discuss.

Wait outside."

Old Mother Knucklebone looked at Arthur. One wrinkled lid dropped over a yellow eye. Behind her skirt, her lumpy thumb pointed upwards.

Arthur bowed and left the room.

Half an hour later, Old Mother Knucklebone shuffled out of the door. There was a crooked smile on her face.

When she saw Arthur, she put her finger to her lips.

"Eat this," she said in a hoarse whisper, scooping out the remains of her jar.

Half a spider wriggled in a blob of treacle.
"And polish your armour till it shines like silver."

"What armour?" said Arthur, reluctantly putting the sticky blob in his mouth. "I don't have any armour."

His mother looked at him. "I hear there's a tournament, today," she croaked.

"It's nothing to do with me," said Arthur. "I never go to tournaments."

"You will, my boy," said his mother, patting the pouch at her waist. "Mark my words, the bones never lie."

But before Arthur could ask her what on

earth she was talking about, there was a crash. It sounded just like a breakfast tray being thrown onto the floor.

The heavy oak door flew open.
"Arthur!" bellowed the King. "Fetch me my clothes and change your own. You will accompany the Royal Household to the tournament!"

3

The Sneeze That Must Be Obeyed

Arthur Knucklebone and George McWhibble stood in an enormous field just outside London and stared. They could barely believe their eyes.

Cardinal Wolsey had hired a thousand craftsmen to build a miniature city of brightly coloured tents, cock-fighting pits, archery butts and a banqueting hall made out of brightly painted canvas.

"Where is the jousting to be held?" asked Arthur.

"Over there," replied George, pointing to a big square of grass surrounded by a red and yellow wooden fence. At one end was a stand with benches for the spectators. Down the middle of the square was a wooden barrier decorated with vines and flowers.

Arthur and George pushed through the crowds. The air was hot and smelled of roasting meat and sweet cakes. Everywhere Arthur looked, people were laughing and drinking. There were men wrestling surrounded by others

cheering and shouting. Archers stood in
line and pulled back on their great bows.

He saw
people
squatting
on the
dusty
ground,
betting
pennies

on games of dice. Around them, musicians strummed their instruments. And above them jugglers' clubs tumbled in the air.

"Hurry!" cried George, prodding Arthur in the side. "The King has arrived!"

Arthur turned to see Henry trotting across the field on a white horse. Cardinal Wolsey was by his side surrounded by a group of nervous-looking courtiers. A sea of shining banners fluttered all around them.

At the same moment, another man on a horse appeared. He was dressed from

head to toe in gleaming grey armour. His horse's flanks were hung with a metal skirt and its head was inside an armoured mask with a spike like a unicorn's horn sticking out in front.

Arthur stared at the huge knight on his enormous horse.

"Who's *that?*" he whispered.

"That's Hubert Fluffé," said George. "His horse is called Deathblow."

"Hubert Fluffé?" said Arthur. "What

kind of weedy name is that?"

"The weediest," said George. "And that's exactly why Hubert Fluffé behaves like a savage." George smiled grimly. "He's tough, he even eats onions for breakfast."

"That's *tough,*" agreed Arthur, barely able to drag his eyes away from Hubert Fluffé and Deathblow.

"Some say it was the onions that made him Champion," said George.

"Champion what?" asked Arthur.

George rolled his eyes. "Didn't you know?" he cried. "Hubert Fluffé is the Champion Jouster of All France."

Arthur turned. Something had happened to the sea of fluttering banners and the brightly dressed courtiers.

They were nowhere to be seen.

"It's times like these when I'm *really* glad I'm a jelly maker," muttered George.

A prickle of sweat broke out on Arthur's brow. He began to edge into the crowd.

AAAH CHOOO!

Arthur's heart sank. He recognized that sneeze. He looked up into the red-nosed face of King Henry.

"Arthur," snuffled the King. "I have a *terrible* cold. I don't think I ate enough spiders." Henry sneezed again and made a show of blowing his nose with six handkerchiefs, I just *know* it won't go away before the jousting tomorrow."

The prickle of sweat at Arthur's neck turned into a torrent.

"Of course, I'm *useless* when I have a cold," moaned the King.

"But you're the best and bravest in the land," cried Arthur. "The strongest, the truest, the -"

But the King didn't seemed to be listening. "So in the interests of King and country," continued Henry VIII. "*My* interests, that is -" His voice tailed away and he stared hard at Arthur.

By now the huge shadow of Hubert Fluffé and Deathblow towered over them.

Arthur looked sideways at the group of courtiers on the far side of the fair ground. They all seemed particularly interested in staring at their feet.

"Yes, Sire," he muttered.

"Well done, Arthur!" cried the King, smiling. "I'd knew you'd see it, my way."

"Hubert Fluffé," cried King Henry. "Allow me to introduce Arthur Knucklebone. Recently appointed Jouster to the Royal Household!"

4

A Night of Shining Armour

That night Arthur couldn't eat or sleep
because of the swarm of butterflies that
seemed to have moved into his stomach.

Finally he crept out of bed and slunk
downstairs to the kitchens at Westminster
Palace. George McWhibble was slumped

in a chair with his head on the table.

For a moment Arthur forgot his own troubles. "What's wrong?" he said.

George's face was pale and haggard. "They don't want any of my jellies," he cried. "They want a disgusting French jelly for Hubert Fluffé."

"Who do?" asked Arthur.

"The King and Queen," replied George miserably, "for the tournament banquet."

Arthur wandered outside. Why should he worry about disgusting jellies. The chances of him being at the banquet were almost zero. He looked up at the starry night and sighed.

Arthur turned and saw candlelight flickering at the far end of the stables.

Who could be up at this time of night?

He crept along the wall and peered over

the stable door. In one corner, munching a
pile of new hay, was a glossy brown horse
with a white blaze down the middle of its
head. In the other corner sat a young girl
bent over a suit of armour. She was
rubbing at marks that Arthur thought
looked suspiciously red, and she was
humming a tune the King had made up a
few weeks before. It was a catchy tune.
Everyone at court was humming it.

Arthur racked his brain. What *was* it
called? Something to do with clothes. Blue

doublet, no. Red breeches, green shoes. No. "Greensleeves," muttered Arthur, aloud. "That's it."

The girl looked up. "Who are you?" she asked, putting down her cloth and wiping her hands on her apron.

"Arthur Knucklebone," said Arthur, noticing with dismay the red marks her hands left on the apron. "I'm, I'm Jouster to the Royal Household," he stuttered.

The girl raised her eyebrows. "And *I'm* Queen Cleopatra," she replied. "Just waiting for my barge to be mended."

"Don't make fun of me," said Arthur miserably. "It's true."

The girl stared at him. Then she put her hand over her mouth and burst out laughing. "I'm sorry," she said. "I couldn't help it. My name's Matilda. I'm the daughter of the Polisher of the Royal Armour." She made room for Arthur to sit down. "Come and tell me who you *really* are," she said.

Arthur sat down beside her and told her the whole story.

"And that's it,"

he said finally. "So the only thing I know about horses is what you spread over the garden to make cabbages grow."

Arthur swallowed. Tears started to well up in his eyes. Butterflies started to do cartwheels in his stomach. "Is it true he eats onions for breakfast?" he whispered.

Matilda nodded. "But we won't think about Hubert Fluffé," she said briskly. "Not yet, anyway." Matilda stood up. "First, I shall teach you everything *I* know." She pointed to the horse.

"This is Thunderbolt," she said. "You will be riding him tomorrow." She pointed to the horse's head. "You face that way." She pointed to her legs. "You grip with these." She held up a pair of reins. "You steer with these."

They lugged a saddle onto a low

stone wall and Arthur practised getting on and off it and holding on for dear life.

After that he tried sitting up on Thunderbolt with a big pole in his hand and holding on for dear life.

"That pole's called a lance," explained Matilda. "That's what you use to knock Hubert Fluffé off his horse."

Eventually after watching Arthur for two hours, Matilda decided to tie his feet together under the horse to stop him falling off as soon as he got on.

"Now, we'll talk about armour," said Matilda. "You never know what's going to

happen, so you need armour to protect
you and your horse."

Arthur stared at her. Armour. What was
it Old Mother Knucklebone had said
about armour? He cast his mind back to

the moment his mother came out of the King's bedchamber, to the taste of spider and treacle in his mouth. Her whispered words floated into his head.

Polish your armour until it shines like silver.

It didn't seem to make any sense at all, thought Arthur. "Huh," said Matilda, when he told her, "if I were you, I'd try anything."

So Arthur climbed down from the saddle and the two of them polished the armour until it really did shine like silver.

When Arthur looked up again, the stars had almost faded and the sun was just about to rise. He stood stiffly to his feet.

"I'd better be off, then," he muttered. "See you, um, see you, soon, I hope."

"Good luck," said Matilda, giving the top of his helmet one last hard rub. "Just remember one thing."

Hope leapt in Arthur's chest. Perhaps there was a secret trick Matilda had been keeping back from him all this time. "What is it?" he cried.

"When you can smell the onions on Hubert Fluffé's breath," said Matilda, slowly.

"Yes? Yes?" Arthur was almost shouting.

"Duck," said Matilda in a deadly serious voice.

5

Thunderbolt Knows Best

Two hours later Arthur was strapped inside a suit of gleaming armour and sitting on top of Thunderbolt, whose top half was also covered with armour.

"Good luck, Arthur!" cried George McWhibble.

Arthur was about to ask him how he had got on with the French jelly when a white handkerchief waggled in the spectator stand.

It was the signal for the joust to begin and even if Arthur didn't know what to do, Thunderbolt did. The big brown horse wheeled and trotted down to the starting point at the far end of the square.

Arthur looked out at the blue sky and the bright yellow sun shining in front of him. It was such a lovely day. And so sad that it was going to be his last.

At that moment, the Queen waggled her white handkerchief again.

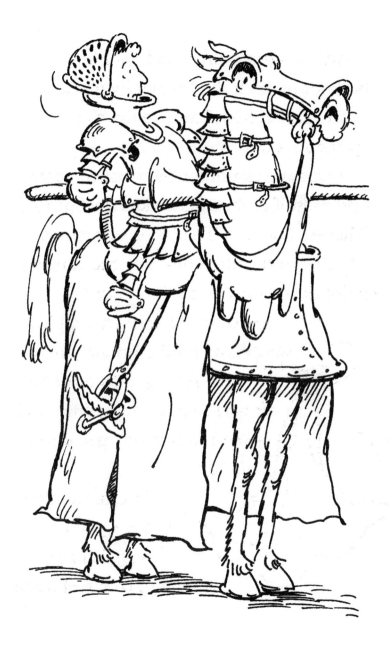

The crowd roared.

Thunderbolt shot forward.

Arthur's visor slammed shut.

The great Jousting Match had begun!

Arthur tucked his lance under his arm.
Then he grabbed his saddle and held on
for dear life.

He could hear the people cheering as he

galloped down the centre of the lists.

And through the slit in his visor, Arthur could see the huge figure of Hubert Fluffé and the metal spike on Deathblow's forehead coming straight at him.

Arthur closed his eyes. It seemed like the only thing to do.

Suddenly a smell of onions wafted into

his visor. Arthur thought of Matilda's last words. He ducked.

At that very second, the bright morning sun, still low in the sky, bounced off the top of Arthur's extra shiny metal helmet.

The shaft of light pierced Hubert's visor and completely blinded him.

To the crowd's total astonishment, Hubert Fluffé, Jousting Champion of All

France and eater of onions for breakfast, thundered straight past Arthur, straight through the red and yellow fence and towards an oak tree with an overhanging branch.

WHACK! Hubert Fluffé slammed into the branch and whirled round like a doll on the end of a rattle.

BANG! CRASH! TINKLE! Hubert Fluffé fell from the branch and landed in a heap.

The Great Jousting Match was over!

Arthur Knucklebone was the new Champion!

A roar of voices exploded over Arthur's head. Hands lifted him down from his horse and carried him shoulder high.

And then Arthur Knucklebone found himself staring into the glittering eyes of King Henry.

"Congratulations, Arthur!" cried the King. "You have served me well. England is great once more. And as King of England, so am I!" The King stood up. "Arthur Knucklebone shall be my guest of honour at the tournament banquet!"

That night, Arthur sat in the middle of

the royal table on a raised platform in the great blue and silver banqueting tent. On his right sat King Henry. On his left sat the Queen. Opposite him, watching everything with wet black eyes sat Cardinal Wolsey.

Arthur had

eaten something from every dish. He had tasted stewed sparrows, roast swan, dishes of pears and rabbits stuffed with walnuts and plums. He had chewed on carp fillets, legs of lamb, necks of partridge and haunches of venison. He had drunk mead, strong ale and

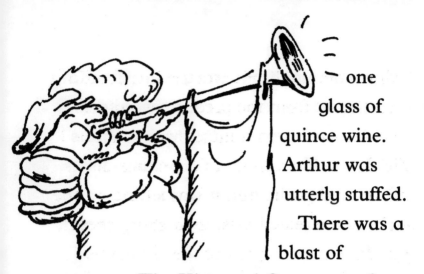

one glass of quince wine. Arthur was utterly stuffed.

There was a blast of trumpets. The King and Queen rose from their chairs and walked across the carpeted floor. Then they stopped on either side of a huge silver salver covered with a domed silver lid.

What on earth could be inside?

Arthur stared at their grinning faces.

Suddenly he remembered George McWhibble slumped over the kitchen table. Something about a French jelly. A really disgusting French jelly.

A horrible cold feeling crept across

Arthur's stomach. He watched as the King lifted the lid from the great silver salver.

Underneath was a huge dragon-shaped jelly. It was breathing a fiery sauce of saffron and garlic and it was sitting on the backs of ten jellied eels, their sharp teeth sparkling in a jelly sea of green onions.

Arthur stared at it. It looked like a really disgusting French jelly. "Eat up, lad!" cried King Henry proudly. "It's all for you!"

Tudor court life

Henry VIII

King Henry did what he
wanted, when he wanted. If
any of his subjects did
something he didn't like, it could
be "off with their heads". The
King was all powerful. Arthur had
to think carefully about what he
could say to the King. And no
matter how unfair, Arthur had to
do what Henry wanted.

Cardinal Wolsey

Cardinal Wolsey (page 16) knew how
powerful Henry was. He tried to
flatter the King by laughing too
much at his jokes. The Cardinal
was the King's chief adviser for
ten years. He did disagree with
Henry when the King wanted to
divorce his wife. Luckily, Wolsey
died before Henry decided to
chop off his head.

Tournaments

These were great events in
early Tudor times. Kings could
show off their jousting skills
and Henry VIII was a brave and
skilful jouster. He jousted for 28
years until he was thrown from his horse. After that,
he never jousted again.

In a jousting match both horse and rider wore
armour (page 33). The horses were often covered in
cloths decorated with their rider's coat of arms. King
Henry's suits of armour can still be seen in the Tower
of London. They are huge and very heavy.

Banquets

These were held after
tournaments, especially
if there was an
important visitor to
court. Tudor
banquets were
enormous. At
one banquet,

King Henry and his guests ate 5 cows, 25 sheep, 10 calves, 15 pigs, 100 hens and pigeons and over 1,000 larks. This does not include the vegetables, beer and wine that was also served. Fish was also eaten in huge quantities. There were freshwater ponds where fish such as carp, tench and pike could be caught.

Puddings were a real favourite in Tudor times. King Henry's cooks made amazing shapes from sugar and jelly. Making a dragon jelly was probably quite easy for them.

Tudor superstitions

 Tudors were superstitious and believed in witchcraft and fortune tellers. Old Mother Knucklebone could do well as long as she told people what they wanted to hear (page 23). Luckily for her, she said the right things to King Henry.